Ricky Ricotta's Mighty Robot
vs. the Jurassic Jackrabbits
from Jupiter

The Fifth Robot Adventure Novel by
DAV PILKEY

Pictures by
MARTIN ONTIVEROS

D1076954

For Joseph and Gracie Ritzert

—D. P.

For Kathy Westray

—M. O.

Scholastic Children's Books
An imprint of Scholastic Ltd
Euston House, 24 Eversholt Street
London, NW1 1DB, UK
Registered office: Westfield Road, Southam, Warwickshire, CV47 0RA
SCHOLASTIC and associated logos are trademarks and/or registered trademarks of Scholastic Inc.

First published in the US by Scholastic Inc, 2002
First published in the UK by Scholastic Ltd, 2002
This edition published 2012

Text copyright © Dav Pilkey, 2002
Ilustrations copyright © Martin Ontiveros, 2002

The right of Dav Pilkey and Martin Ontiveros to be identified as the
author and illustrator of this work respectively has been asserted by them.

ISBN 978 1407 10762 2

A CIP catalogue record for this book is available from the British Library.

Print
Papers used

This is a work of f
of the author's imag

CHAPTER 1

Birthday

One fine morning, Ricky Ricotta
woke up and looked at his calendar.
   "It's my birthday!" he shouted.
"Hooray!"

Ricky ran outside in his pyjamas and woke up his Mighty Robot.

"It's my birthday! It's my birthday!" shouted Ricky. "This is going to be the *best* day ever!"

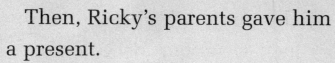

Then, Ricky's parents gave him
a present.

"Wow! A new bike!" said Ricky.
"Thank you, Mom and Dad!"

First, Ricky's parents
cooked peanut-butter
pancakes for breakfast.

Ricky's mighty Robot did
not have a present for Ricky, but
he had an idea.

The mighty Robot flew high into the air and spelled out a birthday message in the sky.

"Thank you, mighty Robot!" said Ricky.

Ricky and his mighty Robot brushed their teeth and got ready to go to the museum.

"We are going to see real dinosaur skeletons today," said Ricky. "This will be the *BEST* day ever!"

"We have one more surprise for you," said Ricky's mother. "Your cousin, Lucy, is coming with us."

"Oh, *NO*!" cried Ricky. "Not Lucy! She is a little *PEST*!"

"She doesn't mean to be a pest,"
said Ricky's father. "She is just lonely.
She has no friends of her own."

"Now you boys be nice to her," said
Ricky's mother.

"Rats!" said Ricky. "This is going
to be the *WORST* day ever!"

CHAPTER 2

General Jackrabbit

Meanwhile, far off in the solar system (about 391 million kilometres, to be exact), even *worse* things were happening on a huge orange planet called Jupiter.

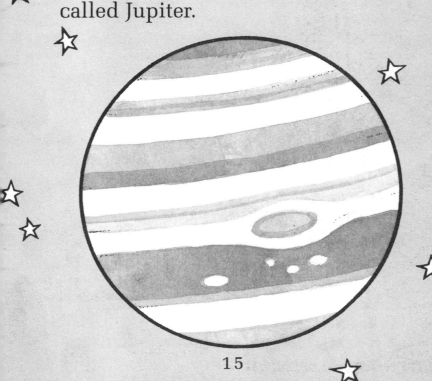

Jupiter was the largest planet in the galaxy, and it was orange because of all the carrots. You see, Jupiter was the home of billions of carrot-loving jackrabbits.

But sadly, they were all
controlled by an evil ruler
named General Jackrabbit.

"I will not be happy until I take over all the planets in the galaxy!" said General Jackrabbit. "And I will start with Earth!"

General Jackrabbit and his two Robo-Rabbit helpers got into a rocket ship and blasted off towards Earth.

CHAPTER 3
An Evil Plan

The first thing General Jackrabbit saw when he got to Earth was Ricky Ricotta's mighty Robot.

"Hmmm," said General Jackrabbit. "If I want to take over Earth, I'll have to destroy that mighty Robot first."

Then he got an evil idea. General Jackrabbit landed his rocket ship on the roof of the museum. . .

MUSEUM

. . .and he sneaked inside.

CHAPTER 4

Lucy the Pest

Meanwhile, Ricky and his family were getting ready to go to the museum. Lucy had just arrived, and she was already being a pest.

"May I have some cake and cookies?" asked Lucy.

"Not until we get back home," said Ricky's mother.

"May I play with the Robot?"
asked Lucy.

"Maybe later," said Ricky's father.

"Will you play princess with me,
Ricky?" asked Lucy.

"No *way*!" said Ricky.

Ricky, Lucy, and Ricky's
parents climbed on to the
mighty Robot's back, and off
they flew to the museum.

"How much longer till we get there?" asked Lucy.

"Soon," said Ricky's father.

"I have to go potty," said Lucy.

"You just went!" said Ricky's mother.

"Can we go ice-skating instead of going to the museum?" asked Lucy.

"*You* can," said Ricky, smiling. "We'll drop you off."

Ricky's mighty Robot giggled.

"*Boys!*" said Ricky's mother. "Be *nice*!"

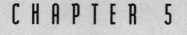

CHAPTER 5

Museum Mishap

When everyone got to the museum, they noticed that something was not right. The Triceratops looked strange. The Pterodactyl was missing something. And the Tyrannosaurus Rex was all wrong.

"The dinosaurs have lost their
heads!" cried the museum guy.
"Don't worry," said Ricky.
"We'll find them!"

Ricky climbed into his mighty
Robot's hand, and the two
friends flew off to look for
the lost dinosaur heads.

Ricky and his Robot looked all around the museum. But they did not think to look on *TOP* of the museum.

MUSEUM

CHAPTER 6
Send in the Clones

Back on the roof of the museum, General Jackrabbit was doing an evil experiment inside his rocket ship.

He took cells from his three stolen dinosaur skulls and put them into his cloning machine. But the dinosaurs were not complete. General Jackrabbit needed more cells. Where could he get them?

"I know," said General Jackrabbit.
"I will add my *own* cells to the
dinosaur cells to make them
complete!" He clipped some hairs
from his fluffy bunny tail and added
them to the dinosaur cells. Suddenly,
the cloning machine began to work.

In a few minutes, three strange-looking eggs rolled out of the cloning machine.

"Success at last!" shouted General Jackrabbit.

Soon the eggs
began to hatch. Out came a
Rabbidactyl, a Trihareatops, and
a Bunnysaurus Rex.

"Perfect!" said General Jackrabbit.

He carried his Jurassic Jackrabbits
up to the nose of his rocket ship and
tossed them out. Then he zapped
them with his Meany Machiney.

ZAAAAAP!

The Jurassic Jackrabbits began to change. They got bigger and bigger, and meaner and meaner.

CHAPTER 7
Jurassic Jack-Attack

Ricky and his mighty Robot could not find the dinosaur skulls, so they flew back to the museum. There they saw a horrible sight.

"Oh, NO!" cried Ricky.
"Dinosaur Bunnies are
attacking the city!"

The mighty Robot set Ricky down
near his family. Then the Robot ran
to fight the evil Jurassic Jackrabbits.

The big, bad bunnies had some terrible tricks in store for Ricky's Robot. . . Like the Crazy Cannonball Creature Crasher. . .

. . .and an unpleasant pile of Prehistoric Power Punchies!

But Ricky's Robot had some tricks of his own. First came the Electro-Reflecto Ejector Protector.

Then came the Telescopic
Two-Ton Turbo Trasher.

And finally the Forcefully Fearsome Free-Flying Fists of Fury!

The Jurassic Jackrabbits moaned and groaned.

"Get back out there and fight, you dino-dummies," cried General Jackrabbit, "or I'll give you something to moan and groan about."

CHAPTER 8

The Big Battle
(IN FLIP-O-RAMA™)

O-RaMa

HERE'S HOW IT WORKS!

STEP 1
Place your *left* hand inside the dotted lines marked "LEFT HAND HERE." Hold the book open *flat*.

STEP 2
Grasp the *right-hand* page with your right thumb and index finger (inside the dotted lines marked "RIGHT THUMB HERE").

STEP 3
Now *quickly* flip the right-hand page back and forth until the picture appears to be *animated*.

(For extra fun, try adding your own sound effects!)

FLIP-O-RAMA 1

(pages 61 and 63)

Remember, flip *only* page 61.
While you are flipping, make sure
you can see the picture on page 61
and the one on page 63.
If you flip quickly, the two
pictures will start to look like
<u>one</u> *animated* picture.

Don't forget to add
your own sound effects!

LEFT HAND HERE

The Jurassic Jackrabbits Attacked.

RIGHT
THUMB
HERE

The Jurassic Jackrabbits Attacked.

FLIP-O-RAMA 2

(pages 65 and 67)

Remember, flip *only* page 65.
While you are flipping, make sure
you can see the picture on page 65
and the one on page 67.
If you flip quickly, the two
pictures will start to look like
<u>one</u> *animated* picture.

Don't forget to add
your own sound effects!

LEFT HAND HERE

Ricky's Robot
Fought Back.

RIGHT
THUMB
HERE

Ricky's Robot
Fought Back.

FLIP-O-RAMA 3

(pages 69 and 71)

Remember, flip *only* page 69.
While you are flipping, make sure
you can see the picture on page 69
and the one on page 71.
If you flip quickly, the two
pictures will start to look like
<u>one</u> *animated* picture.

Don't forget to add
your own sound effects!

LEFT HAND HERE

The Jurassic Jackrabbits
Battled Hard.

RIGHT
THUMB
HERE

The Jurassic Jackrabbits
Battled Hard.

FLIP-O-RAMA 4

(pages 73 and 75)

Remember, flip *only* page 73.
While you are flipping, make sure
you can see the picture on page 73
and the one on page 75.
If you flip quickly, the two
pictures will start to look like
<u>one</u> *animated* picture.

Don't forget to add
your own sound effects!

LEFT HAND HERE

Ricky's Robot
Battled Harder.

Ricky's Robot
Battled Harder.

FLIP-O-RAMA 5

(pages 77 and 79)

Remember, flip *only* page 77.
While you are flipping, make sure
you can see the picture on page 77
and the one on page 79.
If you flip quickly, the two
pictures will start to look like
<u>one</u> *animated* picture.

Don't forget to add
your own sound effects!

LEFT HAND HERE

Ricky's Robot
Won the War.

RIGHT
THUMB
HERE

78

Ricky's Robot
Won the War.

CHAPTER 9

The Meany Machiney

The Jurassic Jackrabbits had been defeated. But General Jackrabbit was not worried. He just zapped the Jurassic Jackrabbits with *another* blast from his Meany Machiney.

The Jurassic Jackrabbits grew
even *bigger* than before . . . and
much, *much* meaner.

The Jurassic Jackrabbits grabbed Ricky's mighty Robot in their terrible paws and began laughing and growling.

"I've got to save my Robot!"
cried Ricky. He climbed on to
the roof of the museum and rang
the doorbell on the rocket ship.

Ding-dong.

The two Robo-Rabbits opened
the door.

"No mice allowed!" said the
Robo-Rabbits. "Jackrabbits
ONLY!" Then they slammed
the door in Ricky's face.

"Jackrabbits only, eh?" said Ricky. Then he got an idea. "I will need everybody's help today," said Ricky. "Especially Lucy's!"

Ricky's family climbed on to
the roof of the museum. Then,
Ricky's mother opened her purse.
She took out two sticks of gum, a
pair of white wool mittens, and
an old white scarf.

Quickly, Ricky's family began dressing up Lucy. The gum made great bunny teeth. . .

. . .and the scarf made excellent
bunny ears. And Ricky sewed the
mittens together to make a fluffy tail.

Finally, Lucy climbed on to Ricky's shoulders.

"Now be careful, you two," said Ricky's father.

"Don't worry," said Ricky. "The good guys always win!"

CHAPTER 10

Ricky and Lucy to the Rescue

Ricky and Lucy went to the rocket ship and rang the doorbell again.

Ding-dong.

When the Robo-Rabbits opened the door this time, they saw a beautiful girl rabbit.

"I'm in love," said the first Robo-Rabbit.

"Ooh-la-laaa!" said the second Robo-Rabbit. "Hubba-hubba!" They took Lucy (and Ricky) into the rocket ship and sat them down at a big table.

"I'm hungry!" said Lucy. "May I have some cake and pie and cookies and muffins and cupcakes and bagels and waffles and doughnuts?"

"Yes, yes, yes!" said the Robo-Rabbits, and they ran off to start baking.

"Now is my chance to look around," said Ricky. He crawled out from under the table and sneaked upstairs.

CHAPTER 11

Upstairs

Upstairs, Ricky saw General Jackrabbit with his horrible Meany Machiney.

"Now, Jurassic Jackrabbits, I want you to destroy that mighty Ro—" General Jackrabbit stopped suddenly and sniffed the air.

Sniff, sniff, sniff.

"Hey!" shouted General Jackrabbit. "Somebody's baking *carrot cake*! What are those silly Robo-Rabbits up to now?"

General Jackrabbit marched
downstairs to see what the problem
was. As soon as he was gone, Ricky
ran to the Meany Machiney and
studied the complex controls.

Ricky turned the dial from BIG, UGLY 'N' EVIL all the way over to LITTLE, CUTE 'N' SWEET. Then he pointed the Meany Machiney at the Jurassic Jackrabbits.

CHAPTER 12

ZAP!

Downstairs, General Jackrabbit was yelling at his Robo-Rabbits when he heard a loud *ZAP*!

"What's going on up there?" he cried.

General Jackrabbit dashed upstairs and saw Ricky blasting the Jurassic Jackrabbits.

ZAP! ZAP! ZAP!

The Jurassic Jackrabbits got littler, cuter, and sweeter with each zap.

"I'LL GET YOU FOR THIS!"
screamed General Jackrabbit. He
grabbed Ricky by the arm and
would not let go.

Suddenly, Lucy appeared at the top of the stairs with a fresh carrot pie.

"Yoo-hoo!" sang Lucy.

General Jackrabbit turned around and. . .

CHAPTER 13

Ricky's Robot
Saves the Day

Ricky's mighty Robot flew down
to the rocket ship to rescue Ricky
and Lucy.

"Now we've got to make things
right again," said Ricky.

First, Ricky's Robot put the
dinosaur skulls back where they
belonged . . . sort of.

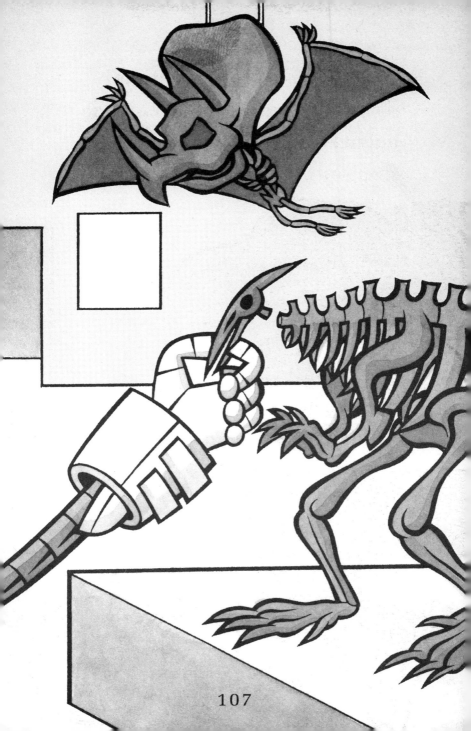

107

Then, Ricky's Robot carefully closed the rocket ship. With one mighty toss, the Robot sent the ship sailing safely back to Jupiter.

"Bye-bye, Robo-Rabbits!"
cried Lucy.

Finally, it was off to jail for General Jackrabbit.

"This has been the worst day ever!" cried General Jackrabbit.

CHAPTER 14

Friends

Soon Ricky and his family got home. It was time for pizza and birthday cake.

"I sure love these cute little Jurassic Jackrabbits," said Lucy.

"Then you should keep them," said Ricky. "Now you'll have little friends of your own!"

"Really?" asked Lucy. "Are you sure you don't want them?"

"I don't need them," said
Ricky. "I already have the biggest
friend in town!"

Finally, Ricky blew out the candles on his cake.

"You know," said Ricky, "this really was the best day ever!"

"Thank you for being so brave today," said Ricky's parents.

"And thank you for sharing," said Lucy.

"No problem," said Ricky. . .

. . ."that's what friends are for!"

HOW TO DRAW RICKY

1.

2.

3.

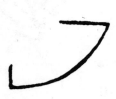

4.

5.

6.

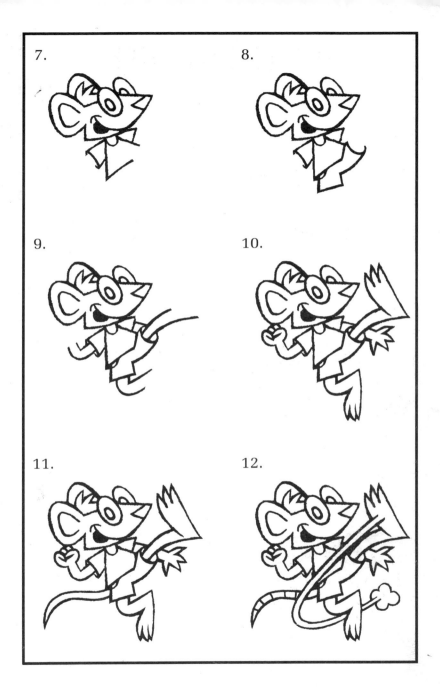

HOW TO DRAW RICKY'S ROBOT

1.

2.

3.

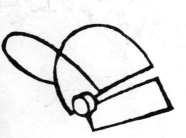

4.

5.

6.

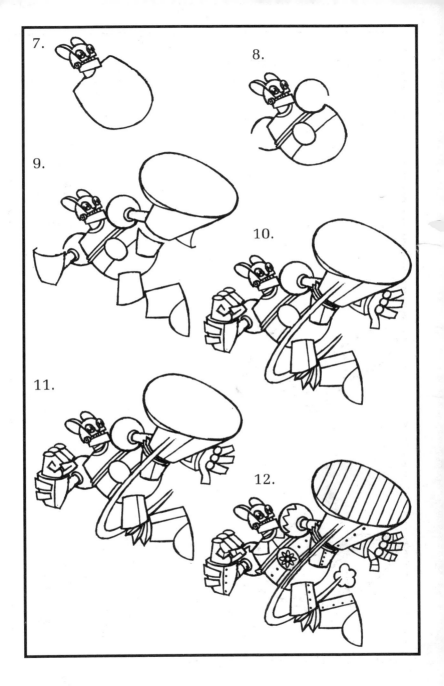

HOW TO DRAW A RABBIDACTYL

1.

2.

3.

4.

5.

6.

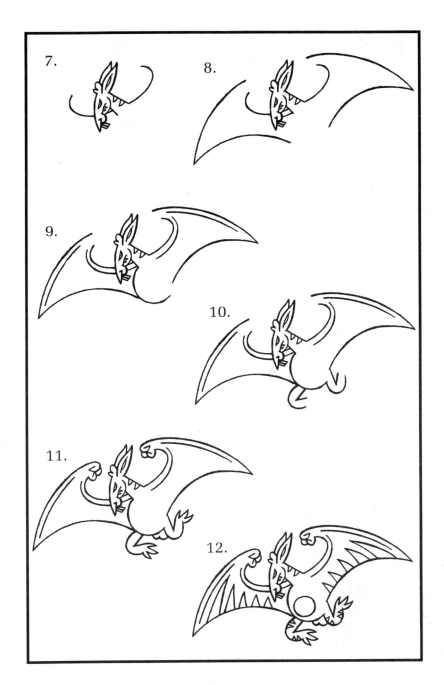

7.

8.

9.

10.

11.

12.

HOW TO DRAW A TRIHAREATOPS

1.

2.

3.

4.

5.

6.

HOW TO DRAW A BUNNYSAURUS REX

1.

2.

3.

4.

5.

6.